Cranky Crocodile Saves the Day

Short Stories, Fuzzy Animals, and Life Lessons

Karma for Kids Books

Norma MacDonald

Cranky Crocodile Saves the Day
Short Stories, Fuzzy Animals, and Life Lessons

Copyright © 2016 Norma MacDonald

First Edition

Published by: Find Your Way Publishing, Inc.
PO BOX 667
Norway, ME 04268 U.S.A.
www.findyourwaypublishing.com

ISBN-13: 978-1-945290-05-3

ISBN-10: 1-945290-05-6

Library of Congress Control Number: 2016944953

Printed in the United States of America.

Dedication

This book is dedicated to all of the people trying to make the world a better place. You are making a positive difference!

"I'm a true believer in karma. You get what you give, whether it's bad or good." ~ Sandra Bullock

"Karma, ahhh. We sow what we reap... We reap what we sow! We reap what we sow. The law of cause and effect. And we are all under this law." ~ Nina Hagen

Table of Contents

About This Book

Welcome to our Karma for Kids Books Series. We are very grateful that you picked up this book. We believe together we can make a positive difference, one child at a time. We strive to instill important life lessons in the lives of young children. We are firm believers in Karma and think that if this simple Law of the Universe is taught to children at a young age, their lives will have the potential to be absolutely amazing.

We once knew a dog named Karma. She was a beautiful, yellow Labrador retriever. It wasn't until after she passed, at 11 years old (God bless her loyal soul.), that we realized just how fitting her name really was.

Karma is indeed a retriever.

Whatever we threw out, Karma was always happy to bring it back to us. It didn't matter what it was, she always brought it back. If we threw out garbage, she'd bring it back without question. If we threw out the most beautiful dog toy, she'd bring it back. It's the same in life. Whatever you send out, is what you will get back. Guaranteed. Every time. Our Karma for Kids Book Series hopes to instill this easy-to-understand Law of the Universe into the lives of children at a young age. The Universe wants to happily bring you all that your heart desires, and it will, effortlessly. But first, you've got to throw out what you want it to bring back to you so that it can! Have fun with this and watch the magic happen. God bless!

Find all of Norma MacDonald's Karma for Kids Books at Amazon.com.

For more of our Karma for Kids books please visit us at:

www.karmaforkidsbooks.wordpress.com
or
www.findyourwaypublishing.com

Other books that we recommend to help children learn important life lessons:

The Many Adventures of Peppy the Emperor Penguin: Short Stories, Fuzzy Animals, and Life Lessons by Norma MacDonald

Lucy Llama and Friends: Short Stories, Fuzzy Animals, and Life Lessons by Norma MacDonald

Ethan Eagle and Friends: Short Stories, Fuzzy Animals, and Life Lessons by Norma MacDonald

Billy Brown Bear and Friends: Short Stories, Fuzzy Animals, and Life Lessons by Norma MacDonald

Humble Heron and Friends: Short Stories, Fuzzy Animals, and Life Lessons by Norma MacDonald

Peter Penguin and Friends: Short Stories, Fuzzy Animals and Life Lessons by Norma MacDonald

Guaranteed Success for Kindergarten; 50 Easy Things You Can Do Today! by Marrae Kimball

Guaranteed Success for Grade School; 50 Easy Things You Can Do Today! by Marrae Kimball

The Secret Combination to Middle School: Real Advice from Real Kids, Ideas for Success, and Much More! by Marrae Kimball

Thank you!

Cranky Crocodile Saves the Day

Short Stories, Fuzzy Animals, and Life Lessons

Karma for Kids Books

Norma MacDonald

Chapter One

You Want a Lift?

Many people call the land down under home and many more people call that place Australia. And when most people think about Australia they think about the hippity hoppity animals called kangaroos. But Australia is full of lots and lots of other interesting animals. Like the cute little koalas. And then there are the dingoes and wombats and wallabies and quolls and crocodiles and echidnas and tasmanian devils, to name a few. And there are also loads of birds and snakes and lizards. Australia is crawling with all sorts of unusual creatures. Some of them are very dangerous. It's hard to know who to trust. And like in most forests around the earth, there's another big danger for the animals in Australia. Fire.

There's an especially dangerous kind of fire that breaks out frequently in Australia—bush fires. Bush fires pose a great danger to the humans and animals in the wild dry land down under. But those raging wildfires pose an especially big danger to the koalas who live in the oily eucalyptus trees.

At the first scent of smoke, every koala knows to move away from the source of the fire as quickly as possible. Kind Koala learned that when he was just a tiny little guy clinging to his mommy's back. They had escaped several fires together before he was old enough to get away on his own. Kind Koala usually stayed quite close to his family. But on this day, he had been chasing a butterfly and before he knew it, he got turned around and lost. That's when he got his first whiff of smoke.

Far from his friends and family, Kind Koala wasn't sure which direction to go. He knew he had to get away, but usually his parents directed him. He wanted to cry because he felt so alone, but he knew that wouldn't help the situation. So he took a deep breath and headed in the direction of the setting sun.

As he moved slowly from limb to limb, he searched the trees for other koalas. But he saw no one. Not even a Magpie or a Parrot or a Raven. All of the birds had flown away. Kind Koala was truly alone. The smell of smoke grew stronger and his little heart began to beat faster in his chest. What was he going to do?

His arms and legs grew tired and he wasn't sure he could keep going. He closed his eyes and remembered how wonderful it felt to ride on his mommy's back. If only he were small again and could be perched on that warm and safe spot. If only he knew where his family was. Why did he get distracted and go off chasing that butterfly? His tummy grumbled and he realized it had been a long time since he'd had anything to eat. So he stopped and pulled off a few leaves from the gum t ree he was sitting in. He continued eating as fast as he could until the empty spot in his stomach was all filled up. Then he took another deep breath and continued moving toward the big orange sun, which was quickly taking its long trip down to the place it disappeared every night.

Tired and sleepy, Kind Koala felt like curling up and taking a nap. But inside his head he could hear his mother's voice saying, "Never, never, never give up." So he continued moving along slowly from limb to limb, branch to branch, tree to tree.

All of a sudden, a voice called to him from somewhere on the ground below. "Hey, what are you doing up there? You're moving way too slow!"

Kind Koala looked down to the forest floor, but he couldn't see anyone. And he knew the danger of trusting anyone he didn't know. "Where are you?" he asked. "And who are you? My mother warned me never to talk to strangers."

"People say I'm strange," answered the voice. "But none of my friends have ever called me stranger. Come on down here and meet me and then we'll be friends and I won't be a stranger to you anymore."

Kind Koala thought the voice sounded friendly, but he still didn't trust him. "What kind of animal are you? How do I know you're not a dingo? Dingoes eat koalas, you know."

"No worries, mate. I'm not a dingo," answered the voice. "And anyway, I have no appetite for koalas. I'm just a regular old grass-eating wallaby."

Kind Koala carefully began to make his way down the tree so he could have a better look. Sure enough, a short and stocky tan-colored hippity hoppity wallaby waited on the ground below. Their eyes met and the wallaby's face broke into a wide smile. "There you are, mate!" He bounced up and down a little bit on his big feet. "My name's Wild, Wild Wallaby."

Kind Koala introduced himself. "Nice to meet you."

Wild Wallaby raised his nose to the smoky air. "It smells like we need to get hoppin'. You want a lift?" he asked.

Kind Koala sighed with relief. The thought of crawling into a pouch and taking a nap while the wallaby hopped to safety was the best idea he'd heard in years. But when he reached the ground, Wild Wallaby patted his back. "Climb on up, mate."

"But don't you have a pouch?" he asked.

"Do I look like a girl?" answered Wild Wallaby. "Only girls have pouches, silly."

Kind Koala blushed in embarrassment as he climbed up onto the wallaby's back. "Sorry. I didn't know."

"No worries, mate. Now let's get hoppin'. Hold on tight!"

So the two of them bounced off into the sunset. It was the wildest ride of Kind Koala's life. Quite different from what he'd experienced during his childhood. His mother never moved fast and his mother never bounced. Wild Wallaby raced through the bush as fast as a shooting star. Kind Koala felt a little scared at first, but once he began to relax, he found the journey rather exciting. Eventually they came out of the trees and moved into a wide open clearing.

When it got dark, Wild Wallaby slowed down and eventually stopped. He turned back toward the bush where they'd just come from and whistled. "Look at that! It's a big one."

Kind Koala blinked a few times. In the far distance, the bush glowed bright red. A tear rolled down his cheek. "I hope my friends and family made it out of there."

Wild Wallaby patted his head. "I'm sure they're just fine, mate. No worries. How about we get some sleep now?"

Kind Koala nodded in agreement and the two of them curled up together and fell into a deep sleep. It didn't seem long before the sun rose and warmed their faces. Wild Wallaby opened his eyes and let out a big yawn. Kind Koala woke up startled. "What was that? Where am I?" It took him a minute before he realized where he was and who he was with.

"Good day, mate! How'd you sleep?"

Kind Koala rubbed his little brown eyes and looked around at the beautiful red rocks that appeared orange with the morning sun. Close by, a creek flowed and the air buzzed with insects. Birds sang their morning songs. Kind Koala felt peaceful, but then he remembered the fire and thought about his family. Where were they this morning? He wondered. Were they somewhere safe? "I'm worried about my family," he said.

Wild Wallaby hopped up beside him. "We'll find them. No worries."

Together they headed down towards the water, but something coming out of the creek stopped them dead in their tracks. Crocodile! What was a saltwater crocodile doing so far from the ocean? Trembling with fear, Wild Wallaby and Kind Koala began to back away slowly. They knew that crocs could never be trusted. "Easy there, Miss

Crocodile," said Wild Wallaby in a shaky voice. "Just carry on with whatever you were doing. We don't want to disturb you."

The croc dragged itself a few steps closer. But something was wrong with the way it was moving. One of its legs trailed behind. "Are you hurt?" asked Kind Koala.

"Isn't that obvious?" growled the croc. "Do you think you dimwits could give me a hand?"

Wild Wallaby and Kind Koala looked at each other and hesitated. They knew they could never trust a saltwater crocodile.

The croc let out a frustrated sigh. "Look you, two. I really need your help. I promise on my mother's life I won't eat you if you help me get other food."

Kind Koala looked again at the crocodile's twisted back leg. It seemed to be broken. "Does it hurt?" he asked, pointing to the injured leg.

The Cranky Crocodile snorted. "Of course it hurts!"

Wild Wallaby motioned Kind Koala to join him in a private spot. The two of them discussed the situation and reached a decision. They would help the Cranky Crocodile, but they would be very cautious not to get too close to her strong jaws and super sharp teeth. She would have to earn their trust.

Chapter Two

Lead by Example

For a solid week Kind Koala and Wild Wallaby had been running themselves ragged trying to round up enough food to keep Cranky Crocodile satisfied. Normally, Saltwater Crocodiles just hid themselves under the water at the edge of the shore to wait for their prey and then quickly attacked. But because of her broken leg, Cranky Crocodile couldn't move quickly enough to catch anything.

But Kind Koala and Wild Wallaby were plant eaters not hunters. They'd never hunted in their lives and they weren't particularly fond of the idea. They felt sorry for the fish and the birds. "Why can't you just eat plants and leaves and fruit and nuts like the rest of us," they asked Cranky Crocodile.

"Are you guys crazy?" she yelled. "I need meat! And lots of it! And if I don't get some soon, I might have to eat you! So get busy!"

Kind Koala sighed. He wondered why she had to be so cranky all the time. They'd been bringing her food three times a day. And not once had she told them thank you. She just complained and asked for more and more food.

Wild Wallaby was getting sick of the crocodile's bad attitude. "I think we should just leave her to manage on her own. We don't owe her anything."

But Kind Koala didn't agree. Her parents taught her that she always needed to treat others the way she wanted to be treated. She explained her feelings to Wild Wallaby. "What if you had a broken leg? Would you want me to leave you behind to fend for yourself or would you want me to take care of you?"

Wild Wallaby scratched his head. "You're right, mate. I'd want you to do the same for me. But I know that you wouldn't be so mean. And I know that you would remember to say thank you!"

"The leg will heal soon and then we can go find my family," Kind Koala lowered his head and his voice softened. "I miss them so much."

"I know, mate," said Wild Wallaby. "We'll track them down soon. I heard some kookaburras chattering this morning. The birds were saying that a ton of animals have relocated all over the bush. A group of ravens have volunteered to try to reunite families who were separated by the fire."

"Really?" asked Kind Koala. "That's great." And with a happy heart, he jumped up on Wild Wallaby's back and the two of them hopped off to try their hands at catching some fish for Cranky Crocodile.

But after several hours, they'd only caught two small fish. As they walked back to where Cranky Crocodile waited for them, they braced themselves for the anger that was sure to come from her. But to their surprise, she ate the snack they'd brought and didn't utter one word of complaint.

The two friends looked at each other and shrugged their shoulders. They didn't know what had changed, but they were glad she was less cranky than usual. Maybe her leg felt better. They both turned to have a closer look.

"What are the two of you staring at?" Cranky Crocodile yelled.

"We just wanted to know if your leg feels any better," said Kind Koala.

"Hmpph. My leg is still a wreck, but at least my belly is full. No thanks to the two of you," she said.

Kind Koala wondered what she'd filled her belly with, but decided he'd rather not know. It wasn't Wild Wallaby and it wasn't himself, so he was grateful. At least they didn't have to worry about catching food for her for a little while.

Tired from the blazing afternoon sun, all three animals found a cooler place in the shade to take a little snooze. They hadn't been asleep for long when the alarming sound of barking brought both Wild Wallaby and Kind Koala quickly out of their slumber.

"Oh no! Dingoes!" cried Kind Koala. "What are we gonna do?"

Wild Wallaby scanned the area to find the location of the dangerous wild dogs. He spotted them coming down the gorge near the creek. Unfortunately, there was nowhere to go. Nowhere to hide. Both Kind Koala and Wild Wallaby began to tremble with fear.

"What are you sissies afraid of?" asked Cranky Crocodile, yawning and showing her massive rows of sharp teeth. "They're just a bunch of brainless puppies."

As soon as the dingoes caught sight of the saltwater crocodile, they took off yelping and running in the opposite direction.

Wild Wallaby and Kind Koala decided it might be a good thing to have the crocodile along for the journey after all, even if she was a little cranky. They approached her and asked if she'd like to stick together for a while.

She gave a full-toothed smirk. "It might not be a bad idea to always have a couple of plump snacks nearby."

Wild Wallaby laughed and hopped off. "You'd have to catch me first."

The Cranky Crocodile snapped her jaws at him. "Don't tempt me."

Kind Koala couldn't tell whether or not she was joking.

The Cranky Crocodile's leg seemed to have healed well enough for her to limp along, but at a very slow pace. "Where are we going?" she asked. "I hope we're headed toward the ocean because that really is the only logical place to go at this point."

"Yes, we're headed to the ocean," said Wild Wallaby. He turned to Kind Koala. "You wanna hop up, mate. I heard that lots of the animals who fled from the fire are meeting up at the ocean."

Kind Koala smiled and climbed up on the wallaby's back. "Thank you. I'm so grateful for the ride.

"You're quite welcome, mate," answered Wild Wallaby.

Cranky Crocodile rolled her eyes. "You guys are way too polite. Who cares about saying thank you all the time."

"It's not just saying the words," said Kind Koala. "It's about the reason behind the words."

"What kind of nonsense are you talking now?" asked Cranky Crocodile.

Kind Koala bounced up and down as Wild Wallaby hopped along." If it weren't for my friend here, it would take me weeks or months to get to the ocean. So I'm grateful for his help. Which is why I said thank you. It's about gratitude."

"Seems like that's something your parents never taught you about," said Wild Wallaby.

"And your mother and father never taught you not to lecture saltwater crocs," Cranky Crocodile snapped.

Wild Wallaby turned and gave Kind Koala a knowing look. They smiled at each other. It didn't seem she'd ever understand the importance of please and thank you. Wild Wallaby decided he would just have to be satisfied and grateful for her protection, even if she was totally rude.

But Kind Koala decided not to give up on Cranky Crocodile. Kind Koala felt happy when people let him know that they liked something he did for them. Maybe by setting a good example-- always telling Cranky Crocodile thank you for everything she did and showing her how much he appreciated her help--maybe just maybe she would see how important it was to show gratitude. It was worth a try. It certainly wouldn't hurt.

Chapter Three

Everyone is Different

The journey to the seashore would take quite a long time because of Cranky Crocodile's injured leg. They moved slowly alongside the river, knowing that rivers always led to the sea. There was always plenty of grass and trees with leaves alongside the water so Wild Wallaby and Kind Koala would have plenty of food to eat. Cranky Crocodile would sometimes slip into the water and wait until something came along that she could grab and eat.

While Cranky Crocodile waited in the river, Wild Wallaby and Kind Koala would relax in the shade of one of the large Boab trees. On this particular day, the sun blazed hotter than ever. By early afternoon all the animals had found a cool place to rest and everything grew very quiet. Kind Koala and Wild Wallaby were very close to falling asleep when they heard what sounded like a chorus of whimpering.

They got up to check it out and what they saw made them both scream out in horror together. "STOP!!!"

Five baby rabbits were huddled together at the bottom of a shrub shaking as Cranky Crocodile limped toward them with her mouth wide open. Wild Wallaby cried out again. "Leave them alone! They're just babies!"

Cranky Crocodile whipped around. "Are you kidding me? This will be the best meal I've had in weeks."

Wild Wallaby hopped over quickly and put himself between the baby rabbits and Cranky Crocodile. "You'll have to eat me first, you overgrown lizard."

Cranky Crocodile snapped her powerful jaws at him. "Get out of my way!"

Wild Wallaby puffed up his chest and stood as tall as he could. "I will not."

"You will," yelled Cranky Crocodile.

"Won't."

"I will eat you!"

Wild Wallaby held his ground. "Go ahead. I dare you!"

Cranky Crocodile moved towards him, her large sharp teeth flashing in the bright sun.

"Noooooooo!" screamed Kind Koala and jumped on Cranky Crocodile's head, covering her eyes with her small paws so she couldn't see where she was going.

Cranky Crocodile swung around and tried to shake Kind Koala off her head, but Kind Koala dug the claws of her feet into Cranky Crocodile's leathery hide.

"Get off of me!" cried Cranky Crocodile. "I will eat all of you."

While the three animals argued, the baby rabbits took advantage of the situation and scurried to safety. When Cranky Crocodile realized they'd gotten away she was furious. "You idiots! Now what am I going to eat?"

Wild Wallaby folded his arms across his chest. "I thought you were going to try to eat us."

"I've lost my appetite for the two of you," she said and turned back and slid into the river.

Wild Wallaby and Kind Koala went back to the shade of the big tree and talked about what had just happened. They realized that eating rabbits was normal behavior for a saltwater croc, but neither of them could stand the thought of it.

"What are we going to do?" asked Kind Koala. "She has to eat and we're not very good at hunting and fishing."

Wild Wallaby scratched his head. "It's a problem."

They both sat in silence for a while, deep in thought.

Kind Koala sighed. "She has to eat. I just can't stand the idea of her eating animals."

"Me, either," said Wild Wallaby.

"Why can't she just eat grass and leaves like us?" asked Kind Koala.

"I reckon crocs just aren't made for that kind of food."

The two of them heard a rustling and looked up. Cranky Crocodile slithered out of the water, a huge fish lodged between her powerful jaws. She shook her head and swallowed it down in a flash. Kind Koala and Wild Wallaby were relieved that she caught something to eat. Maybe she'd be a little less cranky.

"What are the two of you staring at?" she asked.

Neither of them answered.

"Well," she said, limping away. "I suppose it's time we start heading towards the sea again."

Kind Koala couldn't stop thinking about Cranky Crocodile and her live animal diet. Wild Wallaby told him it was just the way it was, but it still didn't seem right to eat animals. He decided to have a talk with her about it. But first he apologized for having jumped on her head and put his hands over his eyes. "I just couldn't stand to see you eat those baby bunnies," he said. "Can you forgive me?"

Cranky Crocodile snorted. "There you go, being all polite again. I'm over it. Now how about I give you a lift. Hop up on my back."

Wild Wallaby had hopped off somewhere near the river and though Kind Koala didn't completely trust Cranky Crocodile, he figured it would be a good chance to talk. So he climbed onto the crocodile's leathery back. "Did you get enough to eat?" he asked, hoping the answer was yes.

"No thanks to the two of you," Cranky Crocodile answered.

Kind Koala scratched his ear. "Have you ever thought about eating a plant diet? You know it's always super easy to find leaves and grass and stuff like that."

Cranky Crocodile stopped walking. "Are you kidding me? That's the silliest thing I've ever heard."

"What's wrong with eating leaves and grass?"

"Nothing if you are made to eat leaves and grass. But do you see these teeth?" she asked, turning her head and opening her mouth. "Do these look like teeth that were made for eating leaves and grass?"

"Maybe," said Kind Koala.

Cranky Crocodile closed her mouth and shook her head. "No. These teeth were made for meat. And that's what I eat. Meat. Some animals were made to eat grass and leaves and some were made to eat meat. That's just the way it is."

"But can't you change?" asked Kind Koala.

"Why should I?" asked Cranky Crocodile. "I like eating meat."

"But what about the animals you eat. Do you think they like to be eaten?"

"What about the grass and leaves you eat. Do you think the trees like having their leaves pulled off?"

Kind Koala had to stop and think about that for a minute. Did the trees feel him pulling off their leaves? Did it hurt the trees? He'd never thought about that before.

"Listen. All of us are made with different needs. All of us have to eat. But not all of us eat the same food. Why do you think there's so much variety? You eat eucalyptus. What if all the animals ate eucalyptus? There wouldn't be enough for everyone, would there?"

"I never thought of it that way," said Kind Koala.

Cranky Crocodile frowned. "So I eat animals. You eat plants. That's just the way it is. Don't judge me."

Kind Koala spent the rest of the afternoon thinking about it. He had been judgmental. Just because Cranky Crocodile ate a different kind of food, didn't make her bad. But Kind Koala still didn't think he could watch her eat. So from that time on, whenever Cranky Crocodile was hunting or eating, Kind Koala would keep his eyes closed.

Chapter Four

Help Those in Need

Some journeys feel like they take forever. The trip to the sea felt like that. Sometimes Kind Koala rode on Wild Wallaby's back. Sometimes he rode on Cranky Crocodile's back. The most fun he had was when he got to hitch a ride with Cranky Crocodile as she plunged into the river. At first he was super scared, but once he got used to it he enjoyed the way the croc rocked gently back and forth as she glided through the gentle water.

Wild Wallaby could go much faster without Kind Koala on his back. Every once in a while, Wild Wallaby and Cranky Crocodile would race to see who could go faster—croc in the water or wallaby on land. Cranky Crocodile almost always won.

Kind Koala missed his family so much. The birds who flew back and forth to the sea told them that a large group of koalas had gathered in a large, grassy area near where the river met the sea. Each day brought them a little closer, but it still seemed to Kind Koala that they'd never get there.

Every afternoon after they'd filled their bellies, the three friends would have a little rest before they continued on with their journey. Wild Wallaby had just closed his eyes when he heard a loud yelping coming from a clump of trees.

"What's that terrible noise?" asked Kind Koala.

Cranky Crocodile opened her mouth into a wide grin. "Sounds like an afternoon snack. You boys stay here and I'll go investigate," she said.

Kind Koala cringed. He decided to stay put. But Wild Wallaby followed the crocodile in the direction the noise had come from. He was very curious about what they might find. The howling continued, so it didn't take them long to find out.

They moved through the bush toward the horrible noise and discovered a young dingo whose leg was caught in some kind of trap. The young wild dog whimpered in pain as it struggled to free itself from the trap. When the poor dog saw Cranky Crocodile moving towards him he got super afraid and his howls grew louder and stronger.

"Calm down, Mate," said Wild Wallaby as he approached the frightened dog.?"

Cranky Crocodile snorted. "Are you telling me I can't eat this lame pup?"

Wild Wallaby sighed. "Is that all you can ever think about is food?"

"Are you saying I shouldn't be able to eat when a great meal is provided that I don't even have to hunt for?" asked Cranky Crocodile.

"I'm saying maybe you should have a little mercy on this young fellow," said Wild Wallaby.

Cranky Crocodile growled. "I am being merciful. Putting this miserable little dog out of his misery is the most merciful thing I could do! You already saved the baby rabbits. Now get out of my way!"

As the two of them argued, the poor dingo, who trembled in fear, tried desperately to free himself from the trap. But the harder he tried, the worse it got. There was no way out. Exhausted, he laid down and panted. "I'm a dead dog," he whined.

Cranky Crocodile and Wild Wallaby continued to argue. Wild Wallaby normally didn't care a hoot about dingoes, but he hated to see an animal caught in a trap and wanted to help. He thought that Cranky Crocodile had no mercy. That she was just interested in an easy meal.

In the meantime, Kind Koala's curiosity got the better of him. He no longer heard the howling and began to wonder what was happening. So he climbed up the nearest tree to see what he could see. From above, he spotted Wild Wallaby and Cranky Crocodile who were still arguing. And then he saw the small dingo huddled into a ball and trembling. Normally koalas are terrified of dingoes, but something told Kind Koala that he didn't need to be afraid of this one. So he moved from tree to tree until he reached the one just above the wild dog. While he scurried from branch to branch, he overheard what Cranky Crocodile and Wild Wallaby were arguing about. It was the same situation they'd had with the baby rabbits. Cranky Crocodile wanted to eat the dingo and Wild Wallaby was trying to talk her out of it.

How many times was this going to happen? Kind Koala remembered the conversation he'd had with Cranky Crocodile about food and her need to eat animals. Maybe fair was fair. Dingoes ate koalas. Crocs ate dingoes. Wild Wallaby argued that the right thing to do was show mercy and help the poor little dog out of its difficult situation. Cranky

Crocodile said that putting the little dog out of its misery by eating it was the merciful thing to do. Kind Koala didn't know who was right and who was wrong. His parents had taught him that to show mercy meant to show kindness or to help someone who was in a very bad situation. The wild dog was definitely in a very bad situation.

Kind Koala noticed that the young dog's leg was caught in a trap. It looked painful. But he couldn't decide whether or not he should help the wild dog or not. After all, dingoes were dangerous. Many koalas had been eaten by dingoes. Why should he help a dingo? Dingoes never showed mercy to koalas. Not that he'd ever heard of.

Kind Koala climbed down the tree until he was just a couple feet above the head of the dingo. Tears dripped out of the young dog's eyes. The dingo looked up at him with those big watery eyes and just whimpered.

The arguing between Wild Wallaby and Cranky Crocodile had heated up. The two of them were shouting at each other. They hadn't even noticed that their koala friend was nearby. Kind Koala wanted to talk with them about what to do, but when he saw the pain in the dingo's eyes, he decided the merciful thing to do was to act immediately. So he crawled down the trap and pulled it apart and released the dingo. The dog was so scared of being eaten by the crocodile that as soon as he was free he whispered a thank you and ran away as quickly as his injured leg would let him.

Kind Koala didn't want Cranky Crocodile to be mad at him, so he quickly climbed up the tree and made his way back to the shady spot by the river and pretended he never knew what happened. But his heart was happy because he'd been able to show mercy to a fellow animal in need. He did what he would've liked done for him.

Chapter Five

Forgiveness

Kind Koala was tired and hungry. They'd already been travelling for over a week and they'd reached an area where there were no eucalyptus trees and not much grass to eat. "How much longer?" he asked as he clung to Wild Wallaby's back.

"A couple days, I think, Mate. Just hang on."

Kind Koala groaned. He was tired of being jostled and bounced around on Wild Wallaby's back. His stomach grumbled all the time and he just wanted to get to the ocean and hopefully find his family. He watched Cranky Crocodile glide into the water and wondered if she'd be willing to let him get up and travel on her back again. At least the ride would be a lot smoother.

Cranky Crocodile was also having a bad day. She hadn't been able to catch anything to eat and her injured leg hurt. So when Kind Koala called out to her from the shore asking for a lift, she pretended she didn't hear him. But then Wild Wallaby started shouting right along with him. She couldn't ignore both of them.

Despite her grumpiness, Cranky Crocodile had grown a little bit fond of the kind little koala. So she decided to come to shore and let him ride on her back. At least for a short time. Little did she know it was a terrible idea.

Kind Koala climbed up on Cranky Crocodiles back close to her head and held on by digging in with the claws on his hands and feet.

"Ouch," cried Cranky Crocodile. "Easy with those sharp claws or I might have to eat you!"

"Sorry about that." Kind Koala let go, but then realized the crocodile was only joking with him. He held on again, but he was careful not to dig in too deep.

For a while, the water was smooth with just a few ripples, but then they entered into a narrow canyon. The current began to move the water along a little faster. Kind Koala's heart also began to beat a little faster. It grew darker because the walls reached so high they blocked out the sun.

Cranky Crocodile maneuvered like an expert through the rocks that stuck out of the water. "Hold on," she said. "We're headed through a rough area."

Kind Koala held on tight and closed his eyes. His stomach felt a little queasy. He began to regret his decision not to stay on land with Wild Wallaby. At least on land he didn't risk falling into the water and drowning.

It seemed like forever, until the water smoothed out again. Kind Koala let out a huge sigh of relief.

And then it happened.

Cranky Crocodile forgot she had a passenger.

Her stomach had been rumbling and grumbling for hours, so when she noticed the big fish hovering just a few feet below the surface of the water she didn't think twice. She just automatically dove under the water and grabbed it.

Kind Koala screamed as Cranky Crocodile plunged under the river. He lost his grip on her back and tumbled into the deep water.

Kind Koala didn't know how to swim.

Wild Wallaby heard the scream from the shore. He watched in horror as the disaster unfolded before his eyes. Kind Koala fell into the river. There was nothing he could do to stop it. He felt frustrated and helpless.

As he hopped along the bank of the river, he saw his little friend's head bobbing up and down in the water. He searched the water for any sign of Cranky Crocodile, but she seemed to have disappeared.

Finally, he saw the crocodile's large tail swishing quickly through the water toward Kind Koala. Cranky Crocodile's back came up underneath the koala. He was safe!

"Whooppeee!" cried Wild Wallaby in relief.

Kind Koala coughed and sputtered the water out of his mouth. Once his fear eased up, he was furious. "What were you thinking?" he yelled at Cranky Crocodile. He didn't care if she got mad at him. She had put his life in danger and he was really, really angry at her.

"I forgot you were on my back. Really. I didn't mean for that to happen," said Cranky Crocodile. She seemed genuinely sorry.

Kind Koala shook the water out of his ears. "Take me to shore immediately. I don't trust you anymore. In fact, I don't want to make this journey with you anymore."

So Cranky Crocodile, swam toward shore and left the soggy little koala on the bank where Wild Wallaby waited.

Wild Wallaby shook his head. "I can't believe you almost let our little friend here drown."

"I didn't mean to," said Cranky Crocodile. "It was a mistake. I swear. Please forgive me."

Wild Wallaby and Kind Koala glared at her. Both were having a hard time finding it in their hearts to accept her apology. The three of them stared at each other in an angry silence. None of them knew what to do next. Wild Wallaby finally spoke up and suggested that he and Kind Koala just leave and forget about travelling with Cranky Crocodile.

"But you might need my protection," said Cranky Crocodile. "I hate to think of the two of you being attacked by a pack of dingoes. I want to help."

Kind Koala and Wild Wallaby didn't respond.

A small kookaburra, who was perched in a nearby tree and had seen the whole thing happen, spoke up. "Are you the three who are heading to the seashore to find that koala's family?" the bird asked. They all looked up at the bird who flapped her wings at them. "Well, are you or aren't you?"

"Yes. Yes. Yes. We are headed to the seashore to try to find my family. Have you heard something about them?"

The kookaburra shook her head no. "But if you are going to make it there, you are going to have to listen to that crocodile. I've heard there are several packs of hungry dingoes running around. I suggest you all forget what happened, forgive each other, and make peace."

Cranky Crocodile agreed. "Please listen to the bird. It was an accident and I'm really, really sorry about what happened. Will you please let me protect you?"

Kind Koala and Wild Wallaby looked at each other and nodded. "The bird is right. We need to help each other. We need to make peace."

And so Kind Koala and Wild Wallaby forgave Cranky Crocodile. Which meant they put what happened behind them and didn't mention it again. And the three friends continued their journey to the seashore together.

Chapter Six

Never Give Up Hope

The journey to the sea took three more days. The sun blazed hot in the sky and food was scarce. But they continued the journey with hearts filled with hope. All three of them looked forward to meeting up with friends and family, but Kind Koala was especially concerned since he didn't know whether or not his family had survived the bush fire.

Because they were eager for the journey to end, the three animals hopped and swam toward the sea without stopping all day long. Each night they were so tired, they fell right to sleep and woke up before the sunrise to get an early start.

It was a good thing that Wild Wallaby and Kind Koala forgave Cranky Crocodile and let her continue the journey with them. Every day they met up with at least one mean pack of dingoes, but Cranky Crocodile always frightened the wild dogs away. If it weren't for her help, Wild Wallaby and Kind Koala never would have made it to the sea alive. She was truly their hero.

On the last day of their journey, they knew they were getting close because the air grew breezy and felt heavier, and they sensed the smell of the sea. All three friends grew excited and energized and moved a little bit quicker.

Kind Koala twitched a little bit with nervousness. What if he couldn't find his family? What if they hadn't made it safely out of the fire. He tried to push those thoughts aside. He had hope. And he held onto that hope. He imagined seeing his mother and his father. How he would cling to them. And his brothers and sisters, too. He missed them so much!

When they arrived at the sea, they found absolute chaos. Large groups of different sorts of animals gathered in big groups. Kangaroos, wallabies, and loads and loads of birds all talking at the same time. But when the crowds of animals noticed the three newcomers they fell silent.

No one could believe that a wallaby and a koala were hanging out with a saltwater crocodile. The animals were surprised and scared and fled as far away as they could get from them.

Kind Koala, Wild Wallaby, and Cranky Crocodile tried to get someone to talk to them about where to find the koalas who had fled the bush fire. But no one would speak to them or answer their questions. Everyone just ran away in fear.

"Maybe if I leave you guys and slip into the ocean, you'll get the information you need," said Cranky Crocodile.

And so they said their goodbyes. Kind Koala had tears in his eyes. He glanced over at Wild Wallaby whose face was full of sadness. "See ya round, mate," he said to Cranky Crocodile as he wiped a tear from his eye. "Thanks for all your help."

Kind Koala hopped on Cranky Crocodile and wrapped his arms around her neck and gave her the best hug he could, considering she was so much larger than him.

The crocodile had become a lot less cranky over the past few days and Kind Koala and Wild Wallaby were sad to see her go. But when Cranky Crocodile burst out crying, they were in shock. They didn't know saltwater crocs ever cried. They all embraced one last time and then Cranky Crocodile made her way across the sand and slipped into the sea. Kind Koala waved goodbye. They both wondered if they would ever see her again.

Wild Wallaby put an arm around Kind Koala. "Let's see if we can go find your family."

Now that Cranky Crocodile wasn't with them anymore, the other animals were willing to talk to them. They found out that because there were so few eucalyptus trees to be found, there were small groups of koalas scattered over several miles of the coast. Kind Koala wondered how he'd ever find his family. It could take days. Or even maybe weeks. Yet his hope still ran high. He was eager to find them, but wasn't sure where to start.

When a group of ravens offered to help fly back and forth to the various groups of koalas, Kind Koala's heart rejoiced. He realized he might be able to be with his family before the sun dipped into the sea!

But over the next few hours, many ravens came back with the same response. They couldn't find Kind Koala's family. Nor could they find anyone who had heard anything about them. With each bit of bad news, Kind Koala's heart sank deeper and deeper into sadness.

"Don't give up hope, mate," said Wild Wallaby. "Never give up hope."

But when the sun went down and there was still no news of his family, Kind Koala started to give up hope. He curled up into a ball under a small bush and cried and cried and cried. He was tired and sad. Wild Wallaby tried to make him feel better. He brought him eucalyptus leaves. But Kind Koala refused to eat. Wild Wallaby curled up next to him and sang lullabies to help him fall asleep.

Kind Koala woke up the next morning to the loud caw of a raven. He opened his eyes to find a young raven bouncing up and down in front of his face. "We found your family! We found your family! We found your family!"

Kind Koala rubbed his eyes. He wasn't sure if he was dreaming. And then he saw them. His mother, his father, and all of his sisters and brothers stepped down and around Wild Wallaby's back.

"I told you, mate," he said with a wink. "Never give up hope."

AFTERWORD

Thanks again for picking up this book! You are participating in making our world a better place.

For more of our *Karma for Kids Books* please visit us at:

www.karmaforkidsbooks.wordpress.com
or
www.findyourwaypublishing.com

Find Norma MacDonald and her books online at Amazon.com.

The Many Adventures of Peppy the Emperor Penguin: Short Stories, Fuzzy Animals, and Life Lessons

Lucy Llama and Friends: Short Stories, Fuzzy Animals, and Life Lessons

Ethan the Eagle and Friends; Short Stories, Fuzzy Animals, and Life Lessons

Billy Brown Bear and Friends; Short Stories, Fuzzy Animals, and Life Lessons

Humble Heron and Friends; Short Stories, Fuzzy Animals, and Life Lessons

Peter Penguin and Friends; Short Stories, Fuzzy Animals, and Life Lessons

Other books that we recommend to help children learn important life lessons:

Guaranteed Success for Kindergarten; 50 Easy Things You Can Do Today! by Marrae Kimball

Guaranteed Success for Grade School; 50 Easy Things You Can Do Today! by Marrae Kimball

The Secret Combination to Middle School: Real Advice from Real Kids, Ideas for Success, and Much More! by Marrae Kimball

If you have ideas for stories, please feel free to share and send them to:

Melissa Eshleman
Find Your Way Publishing, Inc.
PO Box 667
Norway, ME 04268
Melissa@findyourwaypublishing.com

www.findyourwaypublishing.com

Thank you!

www.ingramcontent.com/pod-product-compliance
Lightning Source LLC
Chambersburg PA
CBHW070807120626
46557CB00002B/751